Jim Henson's DOG

THE BIG SQ

*Based on "The Big Squeak," written by J.D. Smith, an episode of the television series **Jim Henson's Dog City**™*

Adapted by Richard Chevat
Illustrated by Matthew Fox

A MUPPET PRESS/GOLDEN BOOK

Western Publishing Company, Inc., Racine, Wisconsin 53404

Library of Congress Catalog Card Number: 93-78953 ISBN: 0-307-12845-8 A MCMXCIV

Hi, I'm Eliot Shag. I have the best job in the world. I draw cartoons. My TV show is about Ace Hart, private detective.

Ace Hart is the bravest, smartest hero that ever was. But sometimes even Ace can find himself in a really tight squeeze.

Let me tell you about one of those times. . . .

It started on a quiet day in Dog City. Things were so quiet that Ace Hart decided to settle in for a short dog nap.

Little did he know that Bugsy Vile had just escaped from the dog pound. The nasty gangster was already planning a crime that would have all of Dog City in an uproar.

While Ace was napping, millionairedale Thirsty Howl was at his family mansion, locking up his safe. Inside was the Howl family treasure—the Diamond Dogbone.

"Safe in the safe," he said out loud. "And the only way to open or close *this* safe is by squeaking my secret squeaky toy."

Thirsty gave the toy a squeak, and the safe door swung shut.

Thirsty had just hidden the squeaky toy in a hollow statue when Bugsy and his gang burst into the room.

"Okay, Howl, hand over the squeaky toy," Bugsy shouted. He'd been listening through an open window.

"No way!" said Thirsty. "You'll never find my squeaky!"

"We'll see about that," said Bugsy.

But even though the gang searched the mansion from top to bottom, they couldn't find the squeaky toy.

"We can't stay here. Someone might spot our truck outside," Bugsy finally said. "We'll take Mr. Howl and his safe back to the hideout."

After the safe was loaded onto the truck, Bugsy drove off.

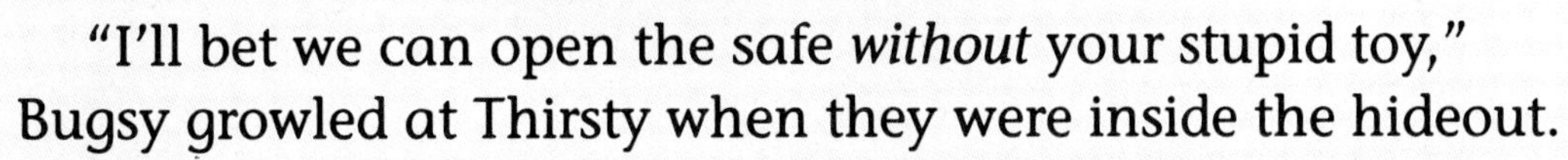

"I'll bet we can open the safe *without* your stupid toy," Bugsy growled at Thirsty when they were inside the hideout.

While Thirsty watched, Bugsy and his gang each tried making a different squeaky noise. One rubbed a balloon, another rocked in a rocking chair, and Bugsy scratched his claws on a blackboard. But the safe wouldn't open.

"This isn't working," Bugsy finally admitted. "We'll just have to steal every squeaky toy we can find and hope one will work."

Bugsy and his gang began on Beagle Street. They grabbed squeaky toys wherever they could.

They stole squeaky toys from sleeping puppies . . .

and right out of bathtubs.

They robbed toy stores . . .

and hijacked squeaky toy delivery trucks.

By the end of the day, there wasn't a single squeaky toy left in Dog City!

Even Ace Hart wasn't safe. When he and Eddie, the newspup, returned to the office after lunch, Ace discovered that his favorite squeaky toy was gone. "Who in the world would want to steal Mr. Quacks?" Ace cried.

"Hey, Ace," Eddie said, holding up his newspaper. "Listen to this. Thirsty Howl's been kidnapped. Maybe the same gang that kidnapped Thirsty stole the squeaky toys."

"Could be," Ace said. "Let's check out Thirsty's place."

Before you could shout "Fetch!" Ace and Eddie were inside Howl Mansion.

"That smell," Ace said, sniffing the air. "I'd know it anywhere! Bugsy Vile has been here!"

"Bugsy!" Eddie yelped in fright. "What if he's still here?" Eddie was so scared that he jumped back and knocked the statue off the table. It fell to the floor—and out popped the hidden squeaky toy.

"Let's see that!" Ace said, beginning to add things up. "Thirsty Howl is missing, and so are all the squeaky toys in Dog City—except this one. And Bugsy was here. I'll bet he *did* kidnap Thirsty and steal all the toys."

"But why?" Eddie asked.

"I don't know," Ace replied. "But it must have something to do with Thirsty's squeaky toy. Eddie, take the toy to my office and keep an eye on it. I'm going to look for Bugsy at the Kitty Kat Club."

While Eddie took the squeaky toy back to the office, Ace headed for the Kitty Kat Club, Bugsy's favorite spot.

"He's bound to show up sooner or later," Ace thought as he walked through the dark alley behind the club.

Ace was right—and the minute Bugsy's boys saw Ace, they jumped him. *Bonk!* Ace felt something hit him from behind, and then everything went black.

When Ace came to, he found himself in Bugsy's hideout. "I see you're back in business," Ace said.

"Yeah, it's the squeaky toy business," Bugsy snarled. "And since I hear you've been nosing around the Howl place, I figure you can tell me where Howl's squeaky toy is. We can't open the safe without it."

"So *that's* why you want it!" Ace said. "Well . . ."

But before Ace could finish, in burst Eddie, holding Thirsty's squeaky toy! Eddie had gone to the Kitty Kat Club to look for Ace and had followed his friend's scent to the hideout.

"My squeaky toy!" cried Thirsty.

"Don't move, Bugsy," Eddie said. "The police are right behind me!"

"Oh, yeah?" said Bugsy with a laugh as he grabbed the toy from Eddie. "I don't see any police."

Eddie pulled a piece of paper out of his pocket. "Uh-oh," he moaned. "I gave the police the wrong address—they're on their way to 750 Bark Avenue instead of 750 Park Avenue!"

Bugsy squeezed the rubber bunny. *Squeak!* The door to the safe swung open.

"Hey, this works just like the remote on my TV," Bugsy said.

"Grab the Diamond Dogbone," cried Bugsy. "Lock these mutts in the storeroom, boys, and let's go celebrate!"

"Can we keep the toys?" asked one of the crooks.

"Sure," said Bugsy. "Take them all with you."

The crooks shoved their three prisoners into the storeroom and pushed the safe in front of the door.

Bugsy's gang gathered up all the squeaky toys. Then they headed for the Kitty Kat Club.

Inside the dark storeroom, Ace tried to come up with a plan.

"Those dirty dogs!" Thirsty whimpered.

"Ace," Eddie said.

"Don't bother me now," said Ace. "I'm thinking!"

"But, Ace," said Eddie. "There's a door here."

Luckily for Ace, Eddie, and Thirsty, the storeroom had a dog door built into it.

Eddie quickly untied Ace and Thirsty. They crawled out onto the sidewalk and ran to the club. Bugsy and his pack were celebrating there.

"Hand over those squeaky toys!" Ace demanded.

"And the Diamond Dogbone," added Thirsty.

"Who's going to make me?" growled Bugsy.

"*They* are," said Eddie. He turned to the door and shouted to the dogs outside, "Sic 'em!"

In the door came an angry mob of Dog City citizens. Ace, Eddie, and Thirsty had rounded them up on their way to the Kitty Kat Club.

"Help!" whined Bugsy. He and his gang were trampled as the dogs of Dog City fetched their beloved toys.

"Hold those crooks!" Ace shouted above the squeaking toys. "The police are on their way."

"I gave them the right address this time," said Eddie.

When the police arrived, they found quite a crowd. The citizens of Dog City were reunited with their squeaky toys, and Thirsty Howl had his Diamond Dogbone.

"I guess that about wraps up the case," said Eddie as Bugsy was hauled off to the pound by the police.

"Except for one thing," Ace said sadly. "My squeaky, Mr. Quacks. I didn't see him anywhere."

"You mean *this*?" Eddie said with a smile, pulling a rubber ducky out of his pocket.

"Mr. Quacks!" shouted Ace. "Where were you?"

"When I saw that Mr. Quacks was about to be trampled, I grabbed him," Eddie said. "Now the case is really wrapped up."

"Thanks, kid. You're all right," said Ace. "Come on, I'll walk you home."

Yes, Ace Hart sure is one tough private detective. No matter how tight a spot he gets into, he always manages to squeak through!